MOG'S BOX

for Helen and Nicholas

MOG'S BOX

by Helen Nicoll
and Jan Pieńkowski

PUFFIN BOOKS

It was Monday morning
Where's my breakfast?

Wait till I've made Owl's lunch
Ooh! bat baps

Tuesday
beetle burger!
Wednesday
vole roll!

Thursday
house mouse samosa
Friday
It's not fair
hot frog!

Why can't I have a lunch box?

So Meg got her cauldron

She put in:

3 bits of wood

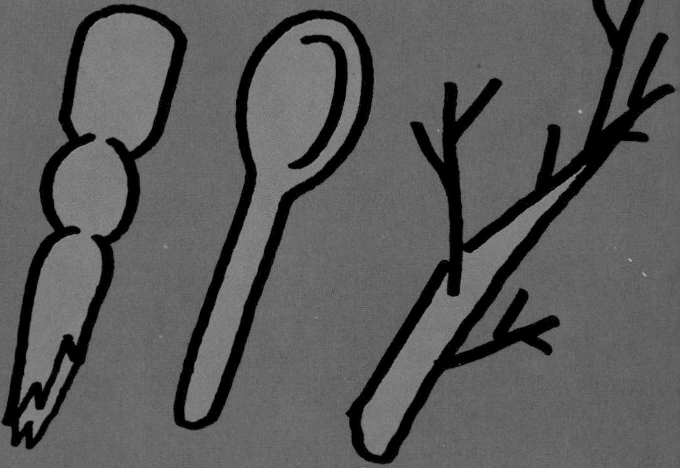

best butter

some nails

55 fly's eyes

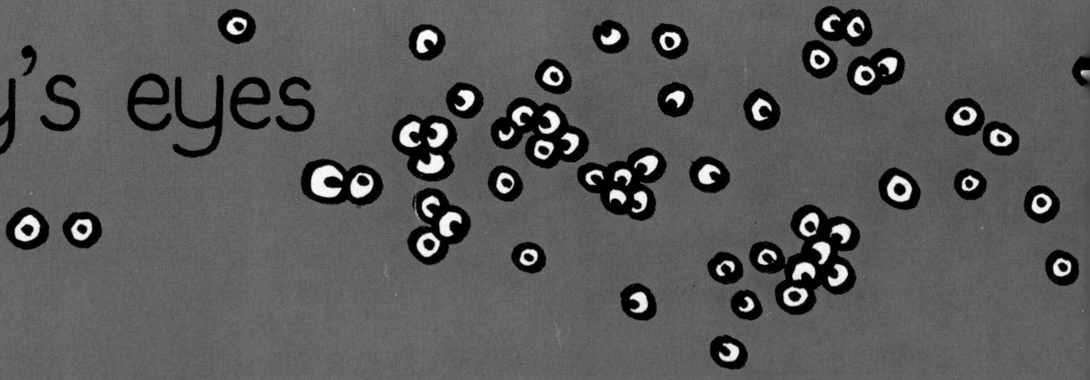

She
made
her
spell

The spell worked

A BIG box appeared

Mog opened the box
?
Is it yummy?
It's green
It's gone bad

It's furry
Must be mouldy
It's moving
Oh dear oh dear

It's a

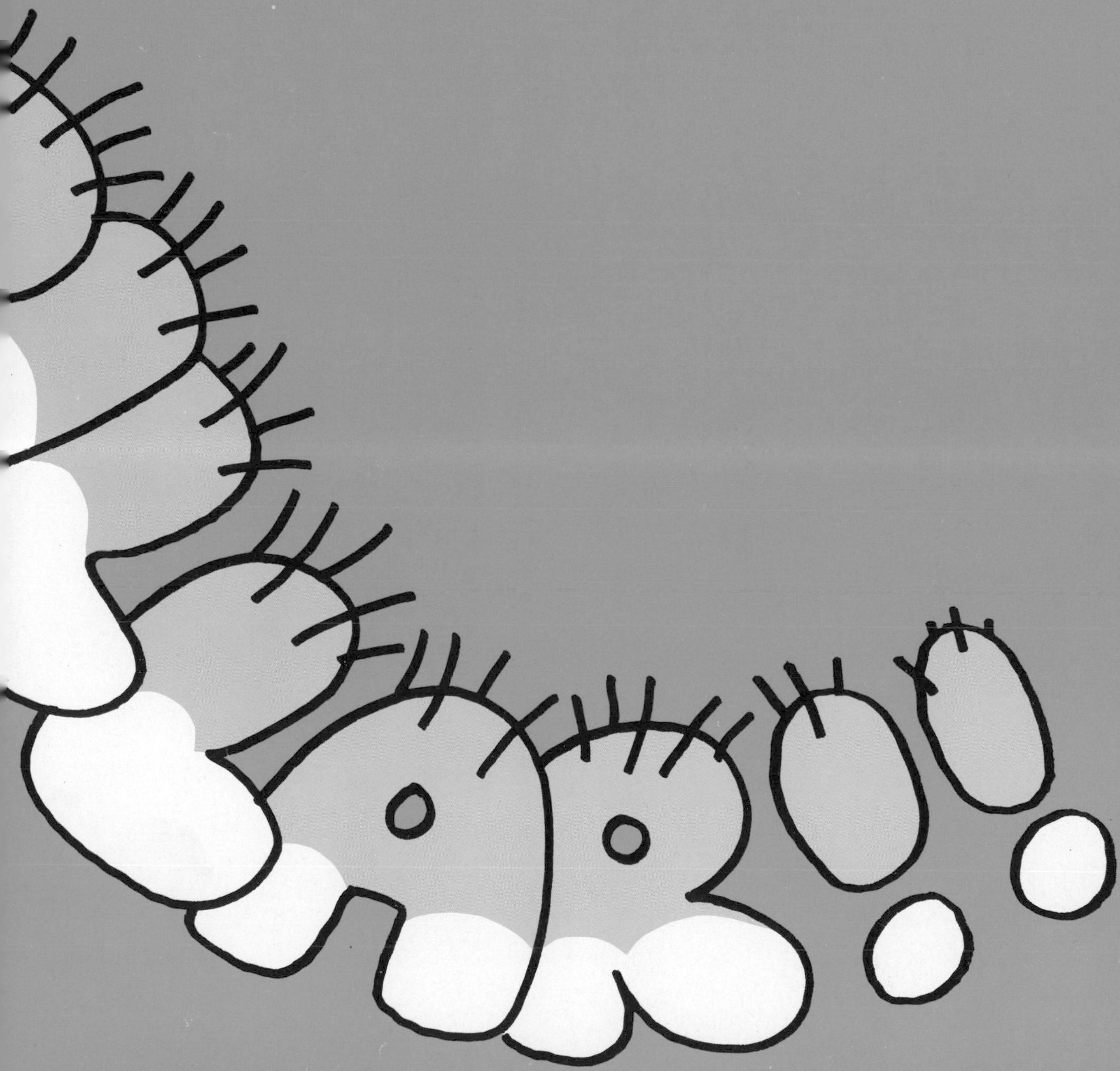

Poor little thing it's hungry

So am I
Do you want a crust?

Meg searched high and low

for the right food

It loves this
MUNCH

The caterpillar grew

bigger and bigger

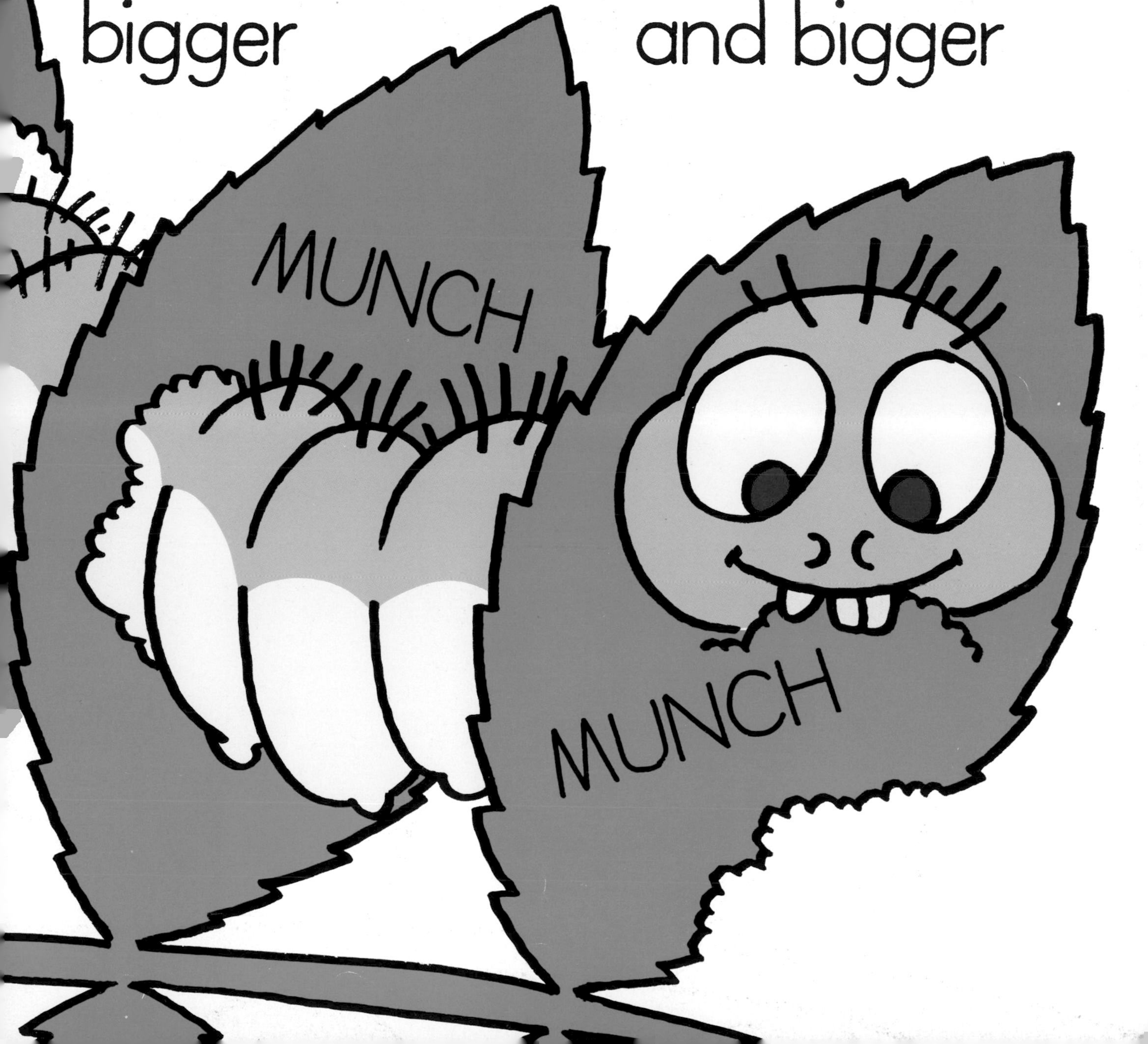

Aah-it's made a cocoon

I'm cold
I'm tired

One fine day...
It's gone

Here it is
It's turned out quite well

Bye bye butterfly
Meg came home

They had tea

After tea

they went to bed

Goodbye!